# The Flamingo Ballerina

With grateful thanks to Anne Marie Ryan.

Illustrations by Nina Jones and Artful Doodlers.

ORCHARD BOOKS

First published in Great Britain in 2020 by The Watts Publishing Group

1 3 5 7 9 10 8 6 4 2

Text copyright © Orchard Books, 2020
Illustrations copyright © Orchard Books, 2020

The moral rights of the author and illustrator have been waived.

A CIP catalogue record for this book
is available from the British Library.

ISBN 978 1 40836 083 5

Printed and bound in Great Britain by Clays Ltd, Elcograf S.p.A
The paper and board used in this book are made from wood from responsible sources.

MIX
Paper from
responsible sources
FSC® C104740
www.fsc.org
FSC

Orchard Books
An imprint of
Hachette Children's Group
Part of The Watts Publishing Group Limited
Carmelite House
50 Victoria Embankment
London EC4Y 0DZ

An Hachette UK Company
www.hachette.co.uk
www.hachettechildrens.co.uk

# The Flamingo Ballerina

**Bella Swift**

# Contents

# Chapter One

"We're all going on a summer holiday!" sang Fifi the flamingo, her voice carrying through the air as she flapped her pink wings. "We're going on *holidaaaaaay!*"

This was Fifi's very first holiday and she couldn't have been more excited. She and her flock were flying all the way from their home in Africa to the south of France, where they would be spending the summer at a beautiful lagoon with lots of other flamingo families.

The flock was flying in a V-shaped formation. Older birds took turns flying at the front, leading the way. Being the youngest flamingo in the flock, Fifi was right at the back. But even with the help from the breeze, it had been a very long trip and Fifi's wings were beginning to ache.

"Are we nearly there yet?" she called to her mum.

"Not much further now," Mum said, craning her long neck back to reply.

"What's it like in France?" she called up to her dad.

"You're going to love it there," Dad said. "The lagoon is gorgeous."

"And the food is just delicious," Mum added. "The prawns are the best I've ever tasted."

"There will be loads of flamingos your age to hang out with," said her big sister, Pinkie, who was flying directly in front of Fifi. "I made lots of friends last summer."

Fifi honked excitedly. She couldn't wait to see the sights, make new friends and try new things. It all sounded AMAZING!

"Look!" she cried, bumping into

Pinkie. "The lagoon!" A glittering blue ribbon twisted and curled through the landscape far below them.

"That's not the lagoon, silly," said Pinkie. "It's a river."

Fifi sighed. She wished they were there already so she could start exploring!

They flew on and on, over sandy beaches, lush green forests and little villages of white houses with orange-tiled roofs. As Fifi was admiring the view below, she suddenly heard a roar. A huge, shiny bird with a pointy nose and lots of eyes was flying straight towards the flamingos!

"What kind of bird is that?" asked Fifi,

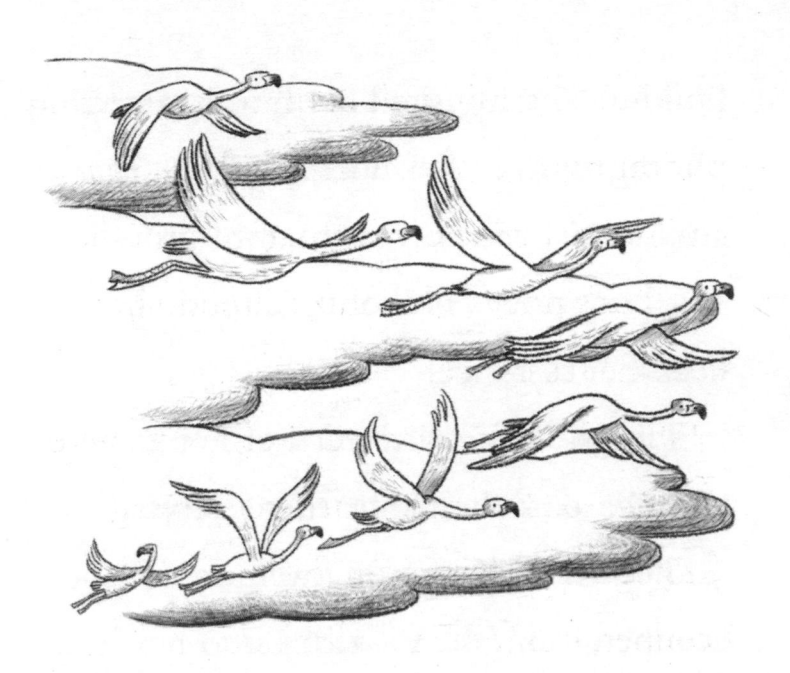

staring in astonishment. She'd never seen
such an enormous creature before!

"That's an aeroplane, feather brain,"
said Pinkie. "It's got humans inside it."

*Ooh, humans!* Fifi had always wanted
to meet a human. She'd seen them from
a distance, of course. Humans on safari

holidays often visited her home, snapping photographs of her flock. *Well, we are a good-looking family*, Fifi thought proudly. But her parents had always made her keep her distance.

"Hello!" Fifi called out as the plane zoomed past them. She turned to try and catch a glimpse of the humans and bumped – *SMACK* – right into her sister again.

"Oops!" said Fifi. "Sorry."

"Mum!" complained Pinkie. "Fifi keeps crashing into me!"

Their mum looked back at them. "Watch where you are going, Fifi. Keep your eyes on the rest of the flock or you'll get lost. Remember what happened last time you wandered off . . . "

As if Fifi needed reminding! A hippopotamus had come to drink at the watering hole where she lived. Fifi had been so curious that she'd wandered off after it – and almost got squashed when it nearly sat on her!

For a while, Fifi tried to do what her mother had said, but it was impossible. There were just too many interesting things to look at on the ground! Strange shapes rose into the air, and tiny things – were they insects? – scurried along on black paths. She could hear beeps and honks coming from them, but they were different from the honking sounds flamingos made.

As the flock flew over the city, a big white building on the edge of town caught Fifi's eye. It was in a park with lots of trees and a big blue lake with a little island in the middle of it.

*I wonder what that is?* thought Fifi,

longing to take a closer look.

Her mum had told her to stay in position, but the lake looked very inviting, sparkling like a sapphire in the sunshine . . .

Curiosity got the better of her, the way it always did.

*I'll just take a teeny tiny peek*, she told herself. She'd only be gone a minute, then she'd catch up with the rest of the flock. Because she was at the back, nobody would even notice her slip away.

Fifi lowered her wings to change direction. Swerving away from her flock, she swooped down towards the glittering lake. She was so eager to get there that she flew too fast and . . .

"Aaarrghh!" Fifi shrieked as she crashed into a tree by the edge of the lake.

Leaves whacked her in the face as she fell down, down, down through the branches, scraping her leg against the rough bark. At the bottom, she crash-landed in the lake with an enormous *SPLASH!*

"Ouch!" groaned Fifi, staggering out of the water on her long legs. She flapped her wings, trying to get back in the air, but there was something wrong. Her left wing hurt and she couldn't seem to fly.

"STOP!" Fifi shouted up to her flock.

"Don't go without me!" But another aeroplane was flying past and the roar of its engines drowned out her cries. Fifi watched in dismay as her flock disappeared into the distance, the pink V-shape getting smaller and smaller and smaller, until finally it was gone.

And with it, her family.

# Chapter Two

*Pinkie's right,* thought Fifi, shaking her head. *I am a feather brain.*

Fifi looked around at this strange place and suddenly became aware of a lovely sound. A tinkling tune, that reminded her of falling rain or a nightingale's song.

Her curiosity growing, Fifi hobbled off,

following the music to a building with
big windows. Through the glass she saw
a flock of pink flamingos, all balancing
on one leg. But as she got closer, Fifi
gasped. These weren't flamingos – they
were HUMANS!

She watched, fascinated, as the humans
in pink leotards balanced on one leg.

They were obviously pretending to be flamingos!

*That's not how you do it*, thought Fifi. She'd just have to show them! She stepped forward but – *BOINK*! – bumped her beak on the window and fell back into the bushes.

Only one of the humans noticed. A girl

with red hair stared at Fifi, her eyes wide. She was so surprised that she toppled over. The other girls giggled and pointed.

"No! No! No!" The music stopped abruptly as a tall, elegant woman dressed in black went over to the girl who had fallen. "Darcy, you MUST keep your balance."

"Yes, Madame," said Darcy. "It's just that I saw a—"

"No excuses!" snapped Madame. "The Grand Show is in just a few weeks. I need you to focus and work hard." She looked around her sternly. "Anyone who does not put in sufficient effort will not return next year." She clapped her hands.

"Everyone — to the barre."

The girls hurried to a wooden
bar that ran around the edge of the
mirrored room. As Madame called out
instructions, they moved their arms and
legs in time to the music.

Fifi watched them, so fascinated she
didn't realise she wasn't alone any more.

"Who. Are. You?" demanded a cold
voice behind her. Fifi spun round in
surprise. Three elegant white birds with
long necks and snowy feathers were
glaring at Fifi with beady black eyes.

The biggest one repeated her question.
"Well?" she demanded. "Who are you?"

"Oh, hi," said Fifi, limping over to

them. "My name is Fifi. What's yours?"
She tried to wave her wing at them,
wanting to be friendly, but it hurt too
much to lift it.

"I ask the questions around here,"
snapped the big white bird.

"You tell her, Odette," said the one on
her left.

"You're the boss," said the one on the
right, nodding.

Odette stretched her long neck
imperiously. "What are you doing here?"

"I was flying with my flock and I
got a bit distracted," explained Fifi. "I
accidentally crash-landed in the water."

The birds flanking Odette sniggered.

"How clumsy," said Odette.

"Where am I exactly?" asked Fifi.

"This is Swan Lake," said Odette. "The clue is in the name. Clumsy, untidy birds like you are not welcome here."

*Ah, so they are swans.* Fifi glanced down. She'd lost some feathers in the fall, and blood dripped from the cut on her leg. She *did* look a bit of a mess. "I've hurt my leg, and my wing," she explained. "I don't think I can fly. I was just watching the humans pretending to be flamingos."

The three swans exchanged confused looks. "Flamingos?" said Odette. "What are you talking about?"

Fifi lifted the wing that wasn't hurt and

pointed towards the building.

The swans burst out laughing.

"Oh, how stupid," Odette sneered. "They aren't pretending to be flamingos – they're ballerinas."

"Ballerinas?" asked Fifi, baffled.

"This is a ballet school, dummy," said Odette. "The humans are learning to become ballerinas."

Fifi was grateful for her pink feathers so the swans couldn't see that she was blushing. "Oh," she said. "I've never met a human before. Or a swan, for that matter."

"We swans are the inspiration for the dancers," bragged Odette, "because we're

so graceful. There's even a famous ballet named after us – *Swan Lake*.

"The school's Grand Show is held every summer on the outdoor stage," she continued, gesturing to a shell-like structure by the side of the lake with a sweep of her enormous white wing.

"People come from all over to watch the ballerinas perform."

"Oh, that sounds wonderful," said Fifi.

Odette looked at Fifi with disdain. "The last thing we need is a scruffy flamingo spoiling the show."

All three swans raised their huge wings and hissed at Fifi.

Frightened, Fifi hobbled away from the lakeside, as fast as her wounded leg could go. She hid behind a bush and peeped out at the swans as they swam around the lake, barely ruffling the water's surface. They were very graceful. But they weren't nice at all!

*What am I going to do?* thought Fifi.

She couldn't fly — and even if she could, she had no idea how to get to the lagoon. There were no other flamingos around, and the swans didn't want to help her. Fifi's wing ached. She desperately wished her mum was there, to kiss it better.

*Will I ever see my family again?* she wondered.

Fifi had never felt so alone. Standing on one leg, she tucked her head under her good wing and cried herself to sleep.

When she woke up, it took a moment for Fifi to remember where she was. *Is this the lagoon?* she wondered, looking out at the lake. *Where are the flamingos?* And then it all came back to her.

Fifi stepped out from behind the bush and looked around. The swans were nowhere to be seen, but there was a noise coming from a nearby weeping willow tree. Limping over, Fifi stuck her head through the drooping branches and saw the red-haired ballerina who had spotted her through the window. No music was playing, but the dancer was balancing on one foot and spinning around so fast she looked like a blur. Fifi started to feel dizzy as she watched her twirl. Wobbling, she flapped her good wing to try and steady herself.

Darcy suddenly stopped spinning and stared at Fifi in surprise. "Oh!" she gasped. "It's you again!"

The ballerina took a step towards Fifi. Fifi backed away nervously. Her mum

had said to stay away from humans.
Maybe this girl was dangerous. Did
humans eat flamingos?

"Please don't eat me!" whimpered Fifi.

The human took another step towards
Fifi.

*Oh no!* Once again, Fifi's curiosity had
got her into trouble. She tried to flee, but
her webbed foot had got caught under a
tree root. She struggled to free herself but
she was stuck!

Fifi quivered as the ballerina moved
closer and closer. She squeezed her eyes
shut, fearing the worst.

"Hold still," said the ballerina softly as
she worked Fifi's foot out from the root.

Fifi opened her eyes again. She was free! Now she could run away – but she didn't. Somehow, she had a feeling she could trust this girl. Her blue eyes were full of kindness and her hands were gentle.

"I'm Darcy," said the ballerina in a low voice. "I know you're scared, but I want to help you." Darcy reached out her hand and stroked Fifi lightly. "Your feathers are so beautiful," she said. "Pink is my favourite colour."

*Mine too!* thought Fifi.

"What should I call you?" Darcy thought for a moment. "I know! I'll call you . . . Fifi! Fifi the flamingo!"

"Yes!" honked Fifi, delighted. "That's my name!" She had no idea how Darcy had guessed, but now she was sure she'd been right to trust her.

"OK, Fifi," said Darcy, smiling at her. "I think you've been in some kind of accident because your leg is bleeding. I'm going to try to bandage it for you."

The dancer untied the pink satin ribbons that wrapped around her ankles and eased off her satin ballet shoes. "Ooh! That feels better," she said, wriggling her toes. "I haven't been on pointe very long," she explained. "Dancing on your toes really makes your feet ache."

Fifi looked at Darcy's feet and winced. The ballerina's toes were bruised and blistered. Weirdest of all, they weren't webbed!

"Ballet looks graceful and elegant," said Darcy, as she tore one of the ribbons off her shoe and gently wrapped it around the cut on Fifi's leg. "But it takes a lot of pain and hard work to make it look that way. Ballerinas are tougher than we look," she said, tying the ribbon into a bow. "The training makes us really strong."

Fifi pecked at the end of the ribbon curiously.

"Don't touch it," said Darcy. "You need

to keep the wound clean so it heals."

"Thank you so much!" honked Fifi.
She looked down at the pink ribbon
around her leg. It made her look a bit
like a ballerina!

"Aww," said Darcy, smiling. "You're
so cute." She frowned. "I wonder where
the rest of your family
is. I've never seen
any other flamingos
around the lake." She
stroked Fifi's feathers
gently. "I bet you
really miss them."

*Oh, I do*, thought
Fifi, nodding.

"I miss my family too," confided Darcy. "At first, when I won a scholarship to travel to France and study at the ballet school it was a dream come true. Madame is one of the best ballet teachers in the world. But the other girls aren't very nice. Everyone is competing against each other – and they're all much better dancers than me. In my old ballet class, I was the best. But here, I'm the worst. One girl, Sabine, is always telling me how rubbish I am."

Fifi remembered how the other ballerinas had laughed when Darcy made a mistake. *But you're a wonderful dancer*, she thought.

"That's why I came out here to practise my pirouettes in secret," said Darcy. "Our Grand Show is coming up soon and I need to get better. I'm worried that if I don't improve, I'll get kicked out of ballet school." She sighed. "Though sometimes I miss my mum and dad so much, I wish I *could* go home."

Tears began to spill out of the ballerina's eyes.

Fifi wished she could make her feel better. She put her good wing around the ballerina to comfort her. As Darcy stroked Fifi's feathers gently, they watched the glowing orange sun set over Swan Lake together. Fifi suddenly realised that she was feeling less lonely. She still missed her family terribly – but at least now she had a new friend!

# Chapter Three

When Fifi woke up under the weeping
willow tree the next morning, she
yawned and stretched. She turned her
neck left and right, bent her long legs,
and then she gingerly opened her wings.
*Ouch!* Her left wing was still sore. Until it
healed, Fifi knew there was no way she

could fly to join her family.

By now, her flock would be at the lagoon, with hundreds of other flamingos. But instead of splashing in the warm water, dining on tasty prawns and making new friends, they would be worried sick. Fifi felt a pang of guilt as she pictured her parents and Pinkie searching high and low for her.

There was a rustle of leaves and Darcy stepped into the shelter of the weeping willow. "Good morning," she said, smiling. "How's your leg?"

"Not too bad," honked Fifi, limping towards her new friend. "But my wing still aches a lot."

Darcy held up some gauze and antiseptic cream. "I got this from the first-aid box so I can change your bandage." She untied the ribbon around Fifi's leg and examined the cut. "Good – it looks like it's starting to heal," Darcy said as she cleaned the wound with antiseptic.

*Ouch!* Fifi made a low grunting noise.

"Sorry, Fifi," said Darcy. "I know it stings a bit." She stroked Fifi's feathers. "I didn't tell anyone at school about you. I'm afraid that if I do, you'll end up in a zoo. I don't like zoos, because I hate to see animals in cages."

Fifi shuddered. Zoos sounded terrible!

"Beautiful creatures like you should be free," said Darcy. "But if you don't get better soon, I'll have to tell Madame so we can take you to the vet."

*No!* thought Fifi, honking in alarm. If someone took her away, she might never get back to her family!

Darcy seemed to understand. "Don't worry, Fifi. I promise I'll look after you." Very carefully, she re-wrapped the wound with soft, white gauze.

After securing the new bandage in place, Darcy said, "I've got to go. I can't be late for class – we have auditions today. Madame is deciding who gets to dance the solo in the Grand Show." She patted Fifi's head. "But I'll be back to check on you later."

"Good luck!" squawked Fifi as Darcy hurried off.

Fifi's tummy rumbled. She was ready for some breakfast. Beyond the branches of the willow tree, the lake shimmered in the morning sunshine. As she peeked out, she noticed Odette and the other swans waddling off the island in the middle of the lake and into the water.

*Uh oh*, she thought. The swans hadn't been very friendly yesterday. But she wasn't going to let a bunch of snooty swans scare her away. Back in Africa her flock had shared their watering hole with lions, cheetahs and hyenas, who were much fiercer than swans!

Remembering what the swans had said about scruffy birds not being welcome, Fifi preened her pink feathers, trying to make herself look tidy. Then she ventured out of the weeping willow and waded into the water. She lowered her neck into the lake and began to drink. *Yum!* The cool water tasted deliciously refreshing as she scooped it up with her beak.

"Hey, Long Legs," shouted Odette, swimming over. "Who said you can go in our lake?"

Fifi pulled her head out of the water.

The swans surrounded her angrily.

"I was really thirsty," said Fifi. "And I haven't had anything to eat for ages." She had hoped the swans would be nicer now that she was looking neater, but they were just as unfriendly as before.

"You obviously haven't had a bath in ages, either," said one of the swans.

"Yeah, you smell bad," jeered the other swan.

"Pink, pink, you stink!" taunted the swans, honking with nasty laughter.

Just then, a blur of brown feathers shot across the sky like a torpedo.

*QUACK! QUACK! QUACK!* A duck with a sleek green head dived down

at the swans. He soared back up in the
sky to escape their pecking beaks, then
swooped down again and again. "Quack
attack!" the duck cried gleefully, flying
at the swans from every angle. The duck
was much smaller than the swans, but he
didn't seem scared of them at all.

Hissing angrily, the swans retreated to

the little island in the middle of the lake.

The duck landed next to Fifi. "Ha! That showed them!" he said, laughing. "*Bonjour*, by the way. My name is Louis."

"Hi," she replied, happy to make a friend. "I'm Fifi. That was really brave."

Louis puffed out his chest. "Those swans think they own the lake, but they don't. My wife and I built our nest here, and we're not going to let those horrible swans scare us off." He gave a loud quack and a lady duck waddled out from some reeds, followed by four fluffy yellow ducklings.

"Aww!" said Fifi. "Your babies are

absolutely adorable."

"*Merci*," said their mother proudly. "I am Marie, and these are our babies — Jean, Jacques, Jules and Josephine."

"*Bonjour!*" quacked Josephine, hopping around Fifi's feet. "Are you a pink duck?"

"No," said Fifi, shaking her head.

"I'm a flamingo."

"Shouldn't you be at the lagoon?" asked Marie, cocking her head to the side. "With all the other flamingos."

Fifi's heart started to pound with excitement. The ducks knew about the lagoon! Maybe they could help her get back to her family! "Yes," she said, nodding. "I had an accident when I was flying there with my flock."

"Oh, you poor thing," said Marie.

"Can you show me how to get there?" Fifi asked them eagerly.

"We can point you in the right direction," said Louis cheerfully. "We flew over the lagoon when we were looking for the perfect place to build our nest."

"I'm hungry," whined Jean.

"Me too," said Jacques.

"Can we have breakfast now?" asked Jules.

The ducklings' mum looked across the lake anxiously. Odette had rounded up a big group of swans, and they were glaring at Fifi and the ducks from the island. "I don't know if it's safe," Marie said. "I'm worried that the swans will hurt you."

"I'm not scared of those mean old swans!" quacked Josephine.

"That's right!" honked Fifi, nodding. "You can't let them bully you."

"But the swans are so big and fierce ..." said Jean nervously.

Fifi thought about the watering hole where she lived. Although there were lots of scary creatures who came there to drink, the flamingos stayed safe because they looked out for each other, honking to warn each other of danger.

"I've got an idea," she said. "Maybe we can team up and help each other?"

"*Ooh la la!*" said Louis. "That's a great idea. I can distract the swans ... "

"... And I can help Marie watch the ducklings!" said Fifi.

"Yay!" quacked Josephine and her brothers noisily.

"OK," said Louis. "Here goes!" He flapped his wings and flew into the air.

"Good luck, *mon amour*!" called Marie.

"Let's go!" Fifi called to the ducklings.

As Louis ducked and dived, bothering the swans, Marie and Fifi led the ducklings into the water for a swim. Fifi soon understood why Marie needed help looking after her babies. The ducklings had a lot of energy – especially Josephine, who kept swimming off to chase dragonflies! Every time a swan got too close, Fifi would honk loudly to warn the ducklings.

The ducklings ate their breakfast, then splashed and played in the water. Fifi tried some pond weed, too. It wasn't as tasty as prawns – but it filled her belly.

"Everyone out!" quacked Louis, flying back to the shore.

Fifi and Marie herded the ducklings out of the water.

"Great teamwork!" Louis said, landing on the bank and giving Fifi a feathery high-five.

Fifi and the ducks sat, hidden by the reeds, letting the sunshine dry their feathers. The little ducklings climbed over Fifi's back, bombarding her with questions.

"Why are your feathers pink?" asked Josephine.

"It's because
of the shrimp
and algae we
flamingos eat,"
explained Fifi.

"Is your poo pink
too?" asked Jean as his
brothers and sister giggled.

"That's not very polite," scolded his mum.

"Do you have any brothers and
sisters?" asked Jacques.

"I have a big sister named Pinkie,"
replied Fifi.

"Do you miss her?" asked Jules.

Fifi nodded. She missed her whole
family a lot. But now she had hope.

The ducks knew the way to the lagoon. And as soon as her wing was strong enough, Fifi would fly there. Nothing would stop her from seeing Pinkie and her parents again soon!

# Chapter Four

"Nap time!" announced Marie, tucking the ducklings into their cosy nest lined with fluffy feathers and velvety moss.

As the ducks dozed, Fifi heard beautiful music drifting out of the ballet school. It floated on the breeze that rippled the lake's water and made the reeds sway.

*I wonder how Darcy is getting on. . .* Fifi knew she should stay out of sight, but she was dying to see how the auditions were going. *I'll just take a quick peek*, she thought to herself.

She hurried over to the ballet school and hid behind a bush so she could watch the ballerinas through the window.

The dancers stood in a line, and as the pianist played, they performed the steps

that Madame called out to them.

"*Plié!*" the teacher said, and the dancers bent their legs at the knees.

"*Relevé!*" They rose high on their toes and stretched their arms above their heads.

"*Sauté!*" Toes pointed, the ballerinas jumped up with their legs perfectly straight and landed on both feet.

When the dancers finished their exercises, Madame clapped her hands

and the dancers hurried over to the barre. "Now that you are warmed up, you will each audition for the solo," she announced. "Remember – I am not just looking for perfect technique. I am looking for an expressive dancer who truly *feels* the music."

As her teacher spoke, Darcy nibbled her fingernails nervously.

One by one, the ballerinas performed. Fifi had no idea how the teacher was going to decide who to give the solo to. They were all so graceful!

"Sabine, you're next," called Madame.

A tall, haughty-looking girl with hair as black as a hornbill's feathers stepped on to the floor. Unlike some of the other ballerinas, she didn't look even slightly anxious as she began to dance. Sabine glided across the wooden floor, performing dizzying pirouettes and gravity-defying leaps. She finished her routine with an elegant arabesque, her leg stretched out behind her. The other ballerinas applauded when she was done.

*Wow*, thought Fifi as Sabine strode back to the barre with a cocky look on her face. *She's really good – and she knows it!*

"Last, but not least," said Madame, "it's Darcy's turn."

Darcy stepped forward, biting her lip

nervously as she waited for the pianist to begin. The audition started well. Darcy's spins and jumps were just as impressive as Sabine's. But there was something special about her dancing. Fifi's heart swelled with emotion as she watched Darcy move to the music.

*I wonder if Darcy's thinking about her family*, thought Fifi.

At the end of her performance, it suddenly went horribly wrong. Darcy leapt high into the air, her legs in a split. But when she landed, she wobbled and landed with a loud thump.

Fifi gasped, hoping her friend wasn't hurt. But the ballerinas at the

barre giggled, and Sabine smirked
triumphantly.

"Oh dear," said Madame, shaking her
head. "Your *grand jeté* needs work, my
dear," she said, helping Darcy up.

Darcy lip trembled and it looked as if
she was trying not to cry.

As the ballerinas filed out of the

dance studio and into the grounds, Fifi
ducked further behind the bushes, hoping
nobody would spot her pink feathers
among the green leaves. She hardly
dared to breathe.

"I'm sure you'll get the solo, Sabine,"
Fifi overheard one of the ballerinas say.

"Well, it definitely won't be Darcy,"
Sabine replied, laughing. "Honestly, she's
so rubbish. Who let her in the school
anyway? She really doesn't belong here."

*That's not very nice*, thought Fifi. Sabine
reminded her of Odette – and not
because of her grace. It was because she
was as mean as the swan! Fifi wanted to
peck Sabine with her beak, but she knew

she had to stay hidden.

Once the coast was clear, she hurried back under the willow tree. Darcy was already there, sitting with her back against the tree trunk, crying her eyes out. Fifi went over to comfort her.

"There, there," she said soothingly, putting her good wing around Darcy.

"Oh, Fifi," Darcy sobbed, burying her face in Fifi's feathers. "It was a complete disaster."

Fifi rubbed her wing against Darcy's cheek, drying her tears with her feathers.

The ballerina wiped her eyes and sniffled. "I get so nervous when I have to dance in front of other people. That's

why I messed up my *grande jeté*." She
shook her head. "If I can't get used to
dancing in front of an audience I'll mess
up at the show."

Fifi loved watching Darcy dance. *You
can dance for me*, she thought. But how
could she make her friend understand . . .

Fifi stood on one leg and raised her

wings, copying what she'd seen the dancers do through the window.

Darcy watched her, a puzzled look on her face.

*I'll have to try something else.* Fifi spun around and leaped up in the air – hoping Darcy would take the hint.

Darcy's eyes lit up with understanding. "Hey, maybe I should practise in front of you!"

"Yes!" hooted Fifi, flapping her wings.

Darcy scrambled to her feet and brushed off her tutu. Then, under the weeping willow, she did her audition dance again.

As she watched her friend, Fifi

suddenly remembered what Darcy had said about dancing making you strong. Could ballet strengthen her wing, so that she'd be well enough to fly to her family?

There was only one way to find out. . .

Darcy sank into a deep *plié*, and Fifi bent her knees.

The ballerina spun around, and Fifi twirled around too.

Darcy balanced on one leg and stretched her arms out. Fifi stood on one leg and spread her wings.

Noticing what Fifi was doing, Darcy stopped dancing and stared at her in amazement. "I don't believe it!" Darcy exclaimed, laughing. "You're dancing too!"

Fifi nodded her head.

"OK," said Darcy. "If you want to be a ballerina, we'd better start at the beginning." She put her ankles together and turned her feet outwards. "This is first position."

Fifi put her webbed feet together and turned them out.

"Very good," said Darcy. "Now for second position . . . " She moved her feet further apart, and spread her arms out wide.

Fifi spread her feet apart and opened both of her wings. It still hurt to move her left wing, but it wasn't as bad as the day before.

"Excellent," said Darcy, nodding approvingly. "Let's move on to third position . . . " Holding one arm in front of her and the other to the side, Darcy moved her feet so that one was slightly in front of the other.

Fifi just about managed to keep her balance as she copied her.

"This is great!" said Darcy. "Dancing is much more fun when you have a friend to practise with!"

Next, she taught Fifi fourth position. "The heels of your front foot should be in line with the toe of your back foot," instructed Darcy.

*What if you don't have toes?* thought Fifi.

Trickiest of all was fifth position. For
this one, Darcy raised both arms above
her head and placed her feet alongside
each other – but facing opposite
directions.

Fifi tried to get her feet into the right
position, but they got tangled up and –
*WHOOPS!* – she toppled over. Luckily
she didn't land on her injured wing.

"Oh dear," said Darcy, helping Fifi up. "Don't worry," she told her encouragingly. "I know it's difficult. You were doing really well."

Fifi attempted fifth position again – and this time she didn't fall over.

"Hurrah!" cheered Darcy. "You'll be a flamingo ballerina in no time!"

# Chapter Five

Every day for the next week, Darcy practised under the weeping willow once her own classes were over for the day. And everything that Darcy did, Fifi did too.

On Monday, Darcy worked on her pirouettes. But spinning made Fifi feel

dizzy. Every time she twirled around,
her tummy churned and she began to
wobble.

"Whoa!" said Darcy, running over to
steady her.

Fifi felt like the whole world was
spinning!

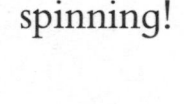

"You need to pick
something to focus on,"
said Darcy. "That will
stop you from getting
so dizzy."

Fifi tried again,
focussing on the tree
trunk as she spinned.
It worked!

On Tuesday, Darcy seemed glum. "Sabine got the solo," she told Fifi, sighing. "No surprises there."

Fifi gave Darcy a feathery hug to comfort her. But she knew Darcy couldn't give up. "Go on," she honked, nudging Darcy with her beak. "You've got to keep practising."

"OK, OK," laughed Darcy, ruffling Fifi's feathers fondly. "You're even tougher on me than Madame!" She began to practise her arabesques.

Fifi soon got the hang of them, too, stretching one long leg straight out behind her.

"Very good," said Darcy, moving Fifi's

leg a bit, to correct her position.

On Wednesday, Darcy worked on *assemblés* – little jumps in the air.

*These are hard,* thought Fifi, trying to land with her feet crossed, the way Darcy did. Even though Fifi kept getting muddled up, Darcy never lost patience with her.

"Well done!" said Darcy, clapping when Fifi finally got it right. "You're a natural!"

Fifi honked with glee and did a little jump for joy.

On Thursday, the ballerina was beaming when she arrived under the tree. "Guess what?" she said, practically bursting with excitement. "Madame praised me in class today. She said my dancing is really coming along!"

"Hurrah!" honked Fifi, flapping her wings excitedly. She was so happy for her friend!

"I think practising with you is helping me improve."

The dancing was helping Fifi, too. She could feel her injured wing getting stronger every day.

On Friday, they worked on *grande jetés*. "These are really hard," said Darcy. "I usually make a mistake." She demonstrated the jump, leaping into the air with her legs in a split.

Fifi let out a noisy squawk of appreciation and clapped her wings together as Darcy landed perfectly.

Darcy sighed in frustration. "I can do it in front of you, Fifi. So why do I keep messing up in rehearsals? I'm so nervous I'm going to wreck the show."

Fifi nuzzled her head against Darcy's cheek. *You'll be great*, she thought. *I know you will.*

Darcy smiled down at the flamingo. "I guess you're my lucky charm."

By the end of the week, the cut on Fifi's leg had healed. Her wing was feeling much better, too. Soon she would be able to fly again. Fifi couldn't wait to join her family at the lagoon. But she knew she couldn't leave before the Grand Show. Her friend needed her.

Fifi spent Saturday hanging out with her duck friends, because Darcy had rehearsal. The ducklings loved to watch her practise ballet moves.

"Look! I can do ballet!" quacked Josephine, trying to copy Fifi's pirouette. She twirled around and around. "Whoa!" she cried, losing her balance and falling on her fluffy yellow bottom.

"Me too!" said Jean, trying to do a

leap – and landing on top of Jacques.

"Hey!" cried Jacques. "Get off me!"
The two ducklings rolled around and
around in the mud.

"My jumps are the best," said Jules,
hopping up and down.

"No – mine are!" said Josephine.
"Aren't they, Mum?"

"Please don't squabble, children," called
Marie from the nest.

Fifi glanced across the water. The
swans were napping on the little island in
the middle of the lake, their heads tucked
under their wings. The coast was clear!

"Shall we go for a swim?" she
suggested to the ducks.

Marie looked at the swans nervously.
"I'm not sure ... Louis isn't here to help
... "The ducklings' dad had flown off to
explore the other ponds in the city.

"Please, Mummy!" begged the
ducklings.

"It will be fine," promised Fifi. She
wasn't going to let the swans spoil the
ducklings' fun.

"OK, then," said Marie. "You can have
a quick swim."

"Yippee!" the ducklings cheered.

"Last one in the water's a rotten egg!"
quacked Josephine, waddling quickly to
be first in the lake.

Fifi and the ducks played in the water

and gobbled up as much pond weed as their bellies could hold.

They were having such fun splashing around together, that Fifi didn't notice one of the ducklings swim off. She counted the ducklings' heads – *one, two, three* ... Where was Josephine?

Turning around, Fifi gasped. The duckling was swimming towards the swans' island!

"What are you doing, Josephine?" she called.

"I want to see what it's like on the island," the duckling quacked.

*Oh no!* thought Fifi. She longed to take a look around the island, too – but she knew this was asking for trouble! Fifi swam across the lake, paddling her feet as fast as she could.

As Josephine waddled on to the shore, Odette and the other swans woke up.

"How dare you come on to our island!" screeched Odette, stretching her beak out threateningly.

Scrambling up on to the island, Fifi spread her wings, shielding the duckling from the swans.

"You again!" said Odette. "What are you still doing here, anyway?"

"Why don't you go pick on someone your own size?" Fifi told Odette.

"Yeah!" quacked Josephine. "Stop

being such a bossy beak!"

The swans gasped in outrage.

"That's it!" hissed Odette. "You're all
banned from Swan Lake!"

"What?" squawked Fifi. "You can't do
that to us!"

"That's not fair!" quacked Josephine.

"The Grand Show is next week,"
Odette snapped. "We don't want you lot
spoiling it!"

*The show!* thought Fifi. She suddenly
remembered that she'd arranged to meet
Darcy after her rehearsal.

"Come on, Josephine," Fifi said,
shooing her into the water again. They
swam back to the side of the lake.

When the ducklings were all safely in
their nest once more, Fifi hurried off to
the weeping willow. But her friend wasn't
waiting for her under the tree. *Maybe she's
still at rehearsal*, Fifi thought. She waited
and waited – but Darcy didn't come. As

the sun began to set, Fifi grew more and more worried. *I'd better check if she's OK.*

Fifi went over to the school building, but the lights in the studio were switched off and there was no music floating out.

Where could Darcy be? It was beginning to get dark, but Fifi knew she had to find her friend. Darcy had said she lived at the school, so she had to be *somewhere* nearby. Sticking to the shadows, Fifi crept around the school and saw a cluster of smaller buildings.

Fifi peered into a window and saw a group of ballerinas eating popcorn and watching a film on television. But Darcy wasn't with them. Now even more concerned, Fifi hurried around the building. She heard a sobbing noise coming from an open window. Peering inside, she saw Darcy crying as she read a piece of paper in her hand.

Fifi let out a squawk of concern and Darcy looked up in surprise.

"Fifi!" she exclaimed, hurrying over to the window and raising the sash. "What are you doing here?"

Darcy helped Fifi climb over the window sill and into her room. Fifi looked around curiously. In the middle of the room there was something big and soft-looking. She supposed it was some sort of human nest.

"Please don't cry," Fifi honked, putting a comforting wing around her friend.

"Oh, Fifi," said Darcy. "I messed up my *grand jeté* in rehearsal. And when I got back to the dorm, someone pushed this note under my door."

Fifi peered at the piece of paper, but the squiggles on it meant nothing to her.

Darcy read it out loud. "It says, 'You are the worst dancer in the whole school. Go home!'"

Fifi gasped. *Who would do something so nasty?*

"It wasn't signed, but I recognise Sabine's handwriting," said Darcy. "She's been even more horrible to me since

Madame praised my dancing."

Fifi let out a squawk of indignation.
Sabine was a bully – just like Odette!
Wanting to show Darcy exactly what
she thought of the nasty note, Fifi ripped
it in half with her beak.

Darcy smiled. "Thanks, Fifi. You always make me feel better."

Fifi looked around Darcy's room in awe. She was actually in a human house! Pinkie would never believe this when she told her . . .

On the walls, there were posters of famous ballerinas. One of them was dressed in a white costume that made her look like a swan.

*Ugh*, thought Fifi. *Someone should write a ballet about flamingos – we're much nicer!*

Fifi pecked at the piles of ballet slippers and leg warmers on the floor. She noticed something fluffy on Darcy's nest and nibbled at it curiously. *Yuck!*

"Don't eat that," said Darcy, taking it out of her beak. "That's my teddy."

Fifi wandered over to the other side of the room. *Hey, those look like me!* she thought, spotting some fairy lights shaped like flamingos draped around Darcy's dressing table. She sniffed a bottle. *Mmm, that smells like flowers!*

"Want to try my perfume, Fifi?" asked Darcy, spraying some into the air.

The perfume tickled Fifi's beak and made her sneeze.

*AAAAACHOOOO!*

There was a knock on the door. Darcy and Fifi stared at each other in alarm. Fifi didn't know the school's rules, but

she was pretty sure the ballerinas weren't
allowed to have flamingos in their
bedrooms – real ones, at least!

"Quick," whispered Darcy. "You need
to hide!"

# Chapter Six

"Just a minute!" called Darcy. She
quickly opened her wardrobe and
shooed Fifi inside. "Don't make a peep,"
she whispered, "or I'll be in big trouble!"

*Oof!* The wardrobe was crammed so
full of pink tutus, it reminded Fifi of
being in the middle of her flock! She

hoped she didn't sneeze again . . .

Peeking through a tiny gap in the doors, Fifi saw Madame come into the room.

"I was worried about you, Darcy," said the dance teacher. "You aren't watching the film with the rest of the girls. Is everything OK?"

*Tell her about the note*, thought Fifi.

"Um, I just wasn't feeling very well," said Darcy.

"Are you sure that's all?" asked Madame, sitting down on Darcy's bed.

"I guess I'm just feeling homesick," said Darcy.

"I understand," said Madame, nodding. "I, too, travelled a long way from home so that I could study at ballet school. I missed my family very much the first year. But to succeed as a dancer, you must make great sacrifices."

"I'm worried that I won't succeed," Darcy admitted quietly. "I'm not as good as the other girls."

"Nonsense. You are a talented ballerina – one of the most expressive dancers I've ever seen," said Madame.

"But I fell again in rehearsal when I did my *grand jeté*."

"Ah, but you got up and tried again. This shows me that you are determined, and not afraid to work hard. A ballerina never stops trying to improve her technique."

As she listened to Darcy talk to her teacher, who seemed much kinder outside the dance studio, Fifi hoped her friend would tell Madame about Sabine. But Darcy didn't say a word about her classmate's bullying.

Eventually, Madame stood to leave. "How pretty," she said, picking up a pink feather. "Where did it come from?"

*Oops!* thought Fifi.

"Oh . . ." said Darcy. "Er . . . um . . . it

must have fallen off my costume."

Luckily, Madame seemed to believe
her. "Get some sleep, my dear," she said
as she left Darcy's room. "Dancers must
work hard – but they also need their rest."

When her teacher had gone, Darcy
hurried over to the wardrobe and flung
open the doors. "Phew! That was a close
call," she said. One of the tutus had
fallen off its hanger and landed around

Fifi. Darcy giggled as she gave her friend a hug. "Now you really look like a ballerina."

Darcy lifted the tutu over Fifi's head and hung it back up in her wardrobe. Then she yawned. "You heard what Madame said, Fifi – we dancers need our sleep. It's time for bed!"

Fifi climbed out of the window and waved Darcy goodbye with her wing. But she didn't go to sleep herself. She was worried about her, and wanted to make sure she was safe. So Fifi stood guard by the window all night long, listening to the gentle snores coming from her friend's room.

With less than a week until the Grand Show, preparations were in full swing the next morning. Workers prepared the outdoor stage by the lake – hanging lights, painting scenery and setting out chairs for the audience.

The dancers were busy, too, practising for the show. After rehearsal, Sabine and some of the other ballerinas relaxed in the sunshine, stretching out on the grass by the lake. Fifi was curious to hear what they were talking about, so she crept behind a bush to eavesdrop.

"Oh, my legs ache," groaned Sabine. "That was such a long rehearsal."

"It went really well, though," said another dancer. "The show is going to be great."

"As long as Darcy doesn't mess it up," said Sabine. "I can't believe she's still here – I thought after I slipped that note under her door she'd take the hint and leave. I'll have to try something else . . . "

"That was kind of mean, Sabine," protested the other dancer. "Darcy's been dancing really well lately."

"She's not as good as me!" snapped Sabine.

Fifi gave a furious honk, then covered her beak with her wing to stifle it. She knew how hard Darcy had been working.

Fifi hurried back to the weeping willow, where Darcy was practising her routine. Unlike the other ballerinas, Darcy didn't stop dancing when rehearsal was over. But even though her dancing was getting better and better, Darcy was still worried about the show.

"I'm used to dancing in front of you, Fifi," said Darcy. "But what about when there are hundreds of people watching me? What if I mess up my jumps in front of the audience?"

Fifi thought for a moment – and then she had a brilliant idea.

She hurried over to the ducks' nest. "Want to see some dancing?" she asked them.

"Yes!" quacked Josephine, scrambling over her brothers to be first.

The entire duck family followed Fifi

back to the weeping willow, quacking excitedly.

"Oh, my goodness!" squealed Darcy. "You've brought your friends to watch me dance!" She stroked their downy feathers as they pecked around her feet. "You're *soooo* cute!"

"Settle down, children," Marie said, and the ducklings obediently lined up neatly in a row and sat down to watch the ballerina dance.

Darcy did her routine for the ducks – and landed her *grand jeté* perfectly.

"*Brava!*" cheered Louis and Marie.

"Hurrah!" quacked the ducklings.

Darcy curtseyed. Then she looked

down at her ballet shoes. "Oops – my ribbon is coming loose. I'd better go sew on a new one."

*Maybe I'll take a nap*, thought Fifi as the ducks wandered off and Darcy went back to her dorm. She buried her head under her wing and was just about to doze off when—

*HONK! HONK! HONK!*

*Oh no,* she thought, suddenly wide awake. *The ducklings must be in trouble.* She really hoped they hadn't invaded the swans' island again . . .

Pushing the willow's drooping branches out of the way, she hurried out and followed the commotion. But the ducks weren't in the water – they were on the outdoor stage!

*Oh dear,* she thought. *This is bad . . .* "What are you doing?" she called to the ducks. If she didn't stop them, they were going to ruin the show!

"We can't go in the lake, so we've gone

on the stage," quacked Louis.

"Look, Fifi!" called Josephine. "I'm a ballerina – just like Darcy!" She twirled and leaped around the stage wildly. Downy yellow feathers flew through the air and got stuck in the freshly painted backdrop.

"Be careful!" cried Fifi. There were nails and sharp tools all over the stage. She didn't want the ducklings to get hurt.

Jean was waddling up and down the piano keyboard, making a dreadful racket.

*PLINK! PLONK! PLINKETY! PLONK!*

Jacques was tangled up in the strings of

fairy lights that the crew were preparing to hang in the trees.

And Jules had waddled into a tray of black paint and left a trail of webbed footprints across the stage.

Meanwhile, Marie and Louis were plucking at the red velvet stage curtain.

"This will make a soft lining for our nest," Marie quacked happily.

"And it's such a lovely colour," said Louis, ripping off a big piece of velvet with his beak.

The swans had surrounded the stage and were honking furiously at the ducks from the water.

"Get off the stage!" hissed Odette.

For once, Fifi agreed with the swans. She knew the ducks didn't mean any harm, but she couldn't let them spoil the show — it was too important to Darcy.

Taking a deep breath, she waded into the water and approached the swans.

"Can we talk?" she asked Odette. "I think we might be able to help each other."

The swan looked down her beak at Fifi. "What are you suggesting?"

"I will keep the ducks from spoiling the Grand Show," Fifi said. "But only if you promise to share the lake with everyone."

Odette swam back to consult with the other swans. As Fifi waited anxiously for their decision, the swans huddled around their leader, murmuring among themselves. Fifi strained her ears, trying to hear what they were saying, but the ducks were making far too much noise.

Finally, Odette swam back over to Fifi. She stopped in front of the flamingo, stretched her neck to its full height and peered down at her haughtily.

"So," Fifi asked the swan nervously. "Do we have a deal . . . ?"

# Chapter Seven

Odette nodded. "We swans will not stop anyone from using the lake."

"Yippee!" cheered the ducks.

"But you'd better not let those pesky ducks wreck the show," warned Odette, glancing up at the stage, where the ducks were quacking noisily and high-fiving each other with their wings. Now they all had splodges of black paint on their feathers.

"They won't," said Fifi. "I pinkie promise." She wasn't going to let anything ruin the Grand Show – not after Darcy had worked so hard. Besides, a flamingo never went back on a pinkie promise!

"Come on, you guys," Fifi called up to the ducks. "Let's get that paint washed off you."

"Woo hoo!" cried the ducks as, one by one, they hopped off the stage and landed in the lake with a splash.

For the next few days, Fifi kept the

ducks entertained – playing games,
teaching them ballet moves and telling
them stories about the other creatures
who lived by her watering hole – so the
crew could get the stage ready without
interruption. Although Darcy and Fifi
were both very busy, they met under the
weeping willow every evening.

"It's the dress rehearsal tomorrow,"
Darcy told Fifi. "I'm so nervous."

"You're going to be great!" Fifi honked,
nuzzling Darcy's cheek.

"I'm excited about the show," said
Darcy. "But mostly, I can't wait to see
my parents."

Fifi had been so busy she'd hardly had
time to think about her own family.
After Darcy went back to her dorm, Fifi
wondered what Pinkie and her parents
were doing right now. Had they given up
on ever seeing her again?

Fifi stretched her left wing. It didn't
hurt at all – not even a twinge of pain.
She hadn't tried to fly yet, not wanting

to risk it, but she was pretty sure her wing was fully healed. Soon, she would soar up into the sky, and join her family at the lagoon.

But not yet. First, she had to help Darcy get through the show.

The next morning, Fifi and the ducks gathered in the reeds by the side of the stage.

"We can watch the dress rehearsal, but you all must be on your best behaviour," Fifi told the ducklings.

"Not a quack out of any of you,"

Marie told her children sternly. She turned to her husband and added, "That goes for you, too."

"We'll be good," promised Josephine. The other ducklings nodded their fluffy little heads in agreement.

"We like Darcy," said Jean.

"We don't want to spoil the show," said Jacques.

Fifi needn't have worried – there were so many exciting things going on that the ducks barely moved a feather as they watched. There was a full orchestra of musicians tuning up, their shiny brass instruments gleaming in the sunshine. Stage crew dressed in black rushed around, performing final light and sound checks. From where the ducks were watching, they could see the backstage area, too. Ballerinas wearing beautiful white tutus were putting on their satin shoes and spraying their smooth, slicked-back buns with hairspray.

"There's Darcy!" Josephine squealed as they watched her warming up backstage.

Putting her wing over her beak, Fifi told the duckling, "Shush!"

Finally, the dress rehearsal began. The orchestra started to play, then a moment later Darcy and her classmates ran on to the stage, their feet turned outwards.

"They walk like us!" quacked Jules.

The ballerinas jumped and twirled in
perfect time to the music. The swans were
right, Fifi had to admit. In their white
tutus, the ballerinas *did* look like swans.
They glided gracefully across the stage
on their tiptoes, their necks long and

their arms outstretched elegantly.

"Darcy's doing really well," Josephine whispered.

Fifi nodded, but she was nervous because she knew what was coming up next – the *grand jeté*!

Because she was the soloist, Sabine was wearing a glittering tiara on top of her hair. While the other dancers ran across the stage, doing their leaps one at a time, Sabine twirled around and around in showstopping spins.

When it was Darcy's turn to jump, Sabine quickly stuck out her leg, tripping her. It all happened so fast that nobody noticed – except for Fifi and the ducks.

*THUD!* Darcy landed on her bottom. She picked herself up and carried on dancing, her cheeks flaming with embarrassment.

"That girl tripped Darcy on purpose!" gasped Josephine.

Fifi nodded grimly. Sabine was so intent on making Darcy look bad, she was willing to spoil the show!

*Well, I'm not going to let her!* decided Fifi. Someone needed to give that bully a taste of her own medicine!

Fifi noticed the ribbon on one of Sabine's ballet shoes trailing slightly. The next time Sabine danced past the edge of the stage, Fifi stretched out her neck and grabbed the end of the ribbon with her beak and *– YANK! –* gave it a quick tug.

Sabine's arms flailed as she tried to keep her balance. She spun wildly across the stage, pitched over the edge and landed in the lake with a loud *SPLASH!*

"Stop!" Madame waved her arms and everything came to a halt. The orchestra stopped playing. The ballerinas stopped twirling.

Soaking wet, Sabine pulled herself back on to the stage. She glared at the other dancers, a puddle forming at her feet. Pond weed dripped from her tutu and her tiara. "It was HER fault," she screamed, pointing at Darcy. "She pushed me!"

The ballerina standing next to Darcy shook her head. "Stop blaming Darcy, Sabine. She was on the other side of the stage."

"Even if she had pushed you, you

would have deserved it after all the mean things you've done to her," said another dancer.

"Yeah – like sending her a nasty note," said the ballerina on Darcy's left.

"And saying rude things to her," said the dancer on her right.

"She tripped her too!" quacked Josephine.

"So . . . " said Madame. "My suspicions were correct. I thought someone was bullying Darcy, but I had no proof." She turned to Darcy. "Is what they are saying true?"

Darcy nodded.

Madame shook her head sadly. "I am

very disappointed in you, Sabine. This school does not tolerate bullying of any kind."

Sabine scowled and stamped her foot. "Darcy doesn't deserve to be here. She can't even do a *grand jeté* properly!"

"Yes, I can!" said Darcy. She ran across the stage and leaped up.

Fifi and the ducklings held their breath as Darcy soared across the stage like a bird in flight. Would she manage to land without falling . . .

Yes!

Darcy landed perfectly, right in front of Sabine. "Told you so," she said, grinning.

The other ballerinas whooped and

cheered. Fifi honked and the ducklings quacking. *Hooray!*

Madame clapped her hands. "I have an announcement!" she said. "Sabine will no longer be performing in the Grand Show. The solo will now be danced by . . . Darcy!"

# Chapter Eight

On the evening of the Grand Show,
the ballet school grounds bustled with
activity as the audience began to arrive.
Fifi knew Darcy would be very busy
getting ready, so she wasn't expecting
to see her before the show. But to her
surprise, the branches of the weeping

willow parted and Darcy stepped under the tree in her white tutu. A crystal tiara glittered on top of her head, and her ginger hair was pulled back into a sleek bun.

"I can't believe I'm actually dancing the solo tonight, Fifi," said Darcy, her eyes shining. "It's a dream come true. I feel so lucky."

Fifi knew it wasn't just because of luck – Darcy had earned the solo with hard work and determination.

"I feel so nervous," said Darcy, chewing on her fingernail. "What if I mess up in front of all of the people out there?"

Fifi rubbed her head against Darcy's

cheek to reassure her. *You won't*, she
thought. *You'll be a star.*

Darcy stroked Fifi's feathers with
trembling hands. "I wouldn't be so
nervous if you were dancing with me
tonight," she said.

*Oh, I wish I could*, thought Fifi. Over the
past few weeks, she had grown to love

ballet. It would be amazing to dance with her friend on stage.

Darcy stooped down and picked up a pink feather that had fallen on the ground. She tucked it into her bun and smiled at Fifi. "Now it will be like you're on stage with me."

Fifi flapped her wings, shooing her friend out of the weeping willow. She didn't want her to be late for the show. "Good luck!" Fifi squawked as Darcy hurried to the backstage area.

Once she was sure that most of the audience had taken their seats, Fifi went over to the reeds by the side of the stage, where the ducks were waiting.

"Just in time," whispered Marie. "The show's about to start."

Fifi gazed around in wonder. Swan Lake looked almost magical in the moonlight. Fairy lights twinkled in the trees around the stage and the sweet scent of flowers filled the balmy night air. Crickets and birds chirped along to the musicians tuning up their instruments.

And the swans glided proudly on the lake's surface, their necks held high.

Fifi shivered with anticipation. She couldn't wait for the show to start!

Finally, the overture began to play and the dancers stepped on to the stage. It was easy to spot Darcy – she was right at the front, her tiara sparkling as bright as stars under the stage lights.

The other ballerinas began to dance around her, their arms bending and swaying like the branches of the weeping willow. But Darcy just stood there on her toes, her arms poised over her head. There was a terrified look on her face as she stared out at the audience, frozen with stage fright.

*Oh no*, thought Fifi. *I've got to help her!*
She spread her wings and took a deep
breath. *Here goes . . .*

Flapping her wings, Fifi soared up
into the air, giving a loud squawk to get
Darcy's attention. A smile of relief crossed
her friend's face when she spotted her.
Fifi landed on top of the sound booth.
Unseen by the audience, but in full view
of the stage, Fifi danced along with
Darcy.

They had practised the routine so
many times Fifi knew all the moves by
heart. Everything that Darcy did on
stage, Fifi did too. They whirled and

twirled in perfect time with each other. As she moved to the music, Fifi thought about leaving Swan Lake. She was excited about seeing her family, but sad to be saying goodbye to her new friends. As they neared the end of the routine, Fifi's tummy tightened. The *grand jeté* was coming up. Darcy had landed it perfectly yesterday – but could she do it again?

Fifi stopped dancing and stared as Darcy jumped into the air and soared across the stage. She landed perfectly, held her pose for a moment, and then dropped into a deep curtsey.

The audience went wild.

"*Brava!*" called Madame.

"Honk! Honk!" cheered the swans.

"Quack! Quack! Quack!" said the ducks.

The audience clapped and clapped as the smiling dancers took their curtain call. Fifi flapped her wings together until they ached. All of the ballerinas had danced well – but none as beautifully or as bravely as Darcy.

After the audience had gone, Fifi went to find the duck family.

"That was amazing!" quacked Josephine. "I'm going to be a ballerina when I grow up."

"Well, if I can be a ballerina, so can

you," said Fifi, laughing.

Odette and the swans swam up to them. *Uh oh.* Would the swans cause trouble again, now that the show was over? But Odette surprised her.

"I'd like to apologise. You're as graceful as any swan, Fifi," said Odette. "Your dancing saved the show. We would like to invite you all to an after-show party on our island to say thank you."

"Can we go?" quacked Josephine.

"Please, please, please!" begged Jean, Jacques and Jules.

"It's past your bedtime . . . " said Marie.

"They were very well-behaved," Fifi pointed out.

"I think they can stay up late, just this once," said Louis.

"Yay!" cheered the ducklings. Fifi watched them fondly as they waddled into the lake and followed the swans across to the island.

"You're leaving us, aren't you?" said Marie quietly.

Fifi nodded. "My wing is better now. I want to join my family at the lagoon."

"Just head east, following the coastline," said Louis. "If you're lucky with the winds, you should get there by dawn."

"We'll miss you," said Marie.

"I'll come back and visit next summer," promised Fifi. "On my way to the lagoon." *But only if I ask Mum and Dad first*, she thought. She'd had an amazing adventure – but she'd definitely learned her lesson about wandering off!

"*Bon voyage!*" called Louis, then he and Marie swam off to join the party.

But Fifi wasn't quite ready to leave yet. There was still one farewell left.

When she reached the weeping willow,

Darcy was waiting for her, clutching a
bouquet of roses.

"Thank you so much, Fifi," said Darcy,
giving her a hug. "I couldn't have done it
without you."

"No, thank you!"
honked Fifi. If it
wasn't for Darcy, she
wouldn't know a *plié*
from a pirouette!

"Well, I'd better
get back to my mum
and dad," said Darcy,
giving Fifi one last
hug. "They're so
proud of me!"

*I'm proud of you, too,*
thought Fifi, watching her
friend disappear into the
night. Darcy had worked
hard to achieve her dreams,
and she'd refused to let a
bully stop her from doing
what she loved.

Then Fifi stepped out
from behind the weeping
willow's branches. Flapping
her wings, she flew into the
night sky, letting the wind
carry her higher and higher.

The warm breeze felt
wonderful rushing against

Fifi's feathers as she soared through the air.

"Goodbye!" she called out, as Swan Lake and the ballet school grew smaller and smaller below her. At last, she was on her way to the lagoon! And the first thing she was going to do when she got there was . . . teach everyone how to dance!

## The End

Have you met Peggy the pug yet?
Here's a sneak peek at
her newest story!

The Pug who wanted to be a Pumpkin

Bella Swift

A big, scary monster stared at Peggy the pug with wild yellow eyes. It roared loudly, showing its sharp teeth. Just as it was about to gobble her up, Peggy woke up from her nap with a start. *Phew!* thought Peggy. *It was just a dream.* But then she opened her eyes and jumped up in fright. Something was coming down the hallway towards her. It wasn't a monster, but it was almost as bad – the vacuum cleaner!

"Sorry, Pegs," called Dad, over the noise of the hoover, "I know you hate this thing, but it's Saturday."

Every Saturday afternoon, Peggy's family did chores. Fleeing from the vacuum cleaner, Peggy ran into the living room. Chloe was cleaning the windows while her older brother, Finn, dusted. Ruby, the youngest, was tidying her toys away.

"I'll help too!" said Peggy, picking up a teddy with her teeth and dropping it into a basket. Of course, to the humans it just sounded like barking.

Mum came into the living room and peeled off a pair of yellow rubber gloves. "The kitchen's finished. How are you lot getting on in here?"

"Nearly done," said Chloe.

Peggy retrieved a train from under the sofa and dropped it on Ruby's lap. Ruby patted her on the head. "Peggy's helping, too."

"Can me and my friends make pizzas tonight?" Chloe asked as she squirted spray on the windows and cleaned it off with a paper towel.

*Mmm, pizza.* Just thinking about it made Peggy drool.

"Of course," Mum said.

"And can we make popcorn and watch a scary movie?" asked Chloe. "*Pleeeease?* It's nearly Halloween."

"Yes," said Mum, laughing. "That's all fine."

"Who's sleeping over tonight?" asked Finn, running the duster over the shelves.

"Ellie and Hannah," said Chloe. "We're sleeping in the lounge with Peggy."

"Yay!" barked Peggy. She and Chloe had been best friends ever since Chloe's family had adopted Peggy from an animal shelter. Peggy loved everyone in her family, but she and Chloe had always shared a special bond.

"Can we stay up really, really late?" Chloe asked.

"As long as you don't keep the rest of us up," replied Mum.

"Me too," begged Ruby. "I want to stay up late."

"You're not allowed," said Chloe. "You're only in reception. You're too little for a sleepover party."

"You can stay up a bit later than usual, Rubes," said Mum, "but this is Chloe's sleepover."

"No fair," Ruby said, pouting.

"You'll have your own sleepover when you're older," Mum promised her.

"You can't bother us either," Chloe told her big brother.

"Don't worry," Finn said, flicking her with the duster. "I don't want to hang out with you and your stupid friends, anyway."

"Good." Chloe stuck her tongue out at him. "Because you're not invited!"

Peggy couldn't wait for Chloe's friends

to arrive. She ran over to the window and jumped up, resting her front paws on the sill. Pressing her flat, black nose against the glass, she looked out at the front garden. The trees were ablaze with red, gold and brown leaves, but there was no sign of Chloe's friends coming down the front path.

"Peggy," sighed Chloe. "I just cleaned that!" She squirted cleaning spray on the window again and wiped away the smudge Peggy's nose had left on the glass. "I want to get it done quickly so I can get ready for my sleepover."

"It's safe to come out, Peggy," said Dad, poking his head round the door.

"I'm done hoovering. Anything else need doing?"

"Nope," said Mum. "That's everything. Great job, everyone."

"Come on, Peggy," said Chloe. "We need to plan for tonight!"

Peggy hurried after Chloe, climbing the stairs as fast as her short little legs could go. Sitting cross-legged on her bed, Chloe took out a sparkly notebook with a unicorn on the cover and began to make a list.

"Pizza . . . pampering . . . popcorn," said Chloe as she wrote.

Peggy thought it all sounded fun – especially the pizza and popcorn! She let out an enthusiastic yip.

"Am I forgetting anything?" wondered Chloe.

Peggy chewed on the corner of Chloe's pillow thoughtfully.

"Ooh, that reminds me!" Chloe said, tugging the pillow out of Peggy's mouth. "We need to have a pillow fight, too!" She quickly added "pillow fight" to her list and gave Peggy a cuddle. "Thanks, Peggy. I don't know what I'd do without you!"

★ ★ ★

At six o'clock the doorbell rang. Barking excitedly, Peggy ran to the door, wagging her tail. "I'll get it!" cried

Chloe, flinging the door open. Her
friends Ellie and Hannah stepped inside,
each holding a backpack and a sleeping
bag.

"Hi, Peggy," said Hannah, crouching
down to give her a pat. "Princess says hi."
Princess was Hannah's pet dog. Peggy
felt a bit sad that Princess wasn't coming
to the sleepover, too, but the playful little
terrier could be a bit naughty. It was
probably for the best.

Read The Pug Who Wanted
to Be a Pumpkin
to find out what happens next ...

# Have you read all these great animal stories by Bella Swift?